Pra
Cora

'Georgina Aboud's stories are both startling and considered. Hers is an important new voice.'

—Cathy Galvin

'Wow. Writing of the highest order. Very few people put words together as beautifully as this.'

—Susannah Waters

'Georgina Aboud has a voice and vision all of her own. She writes prose of rare vividness and lyricism, moving effortlessly between rapture and melancholy, and making startling connections between the past and the present. In *Cora Vincent* she creates a character and a story that speaks strongly to where we are now.'

—Tom Lee

Cora Vincent

Georgina Aboud

CORA VINCENT

First published in 2020 by
Myriad Editions
www.myriadeditions.com

Myriad Editions
An imprint of New Internationalist Publications
The Old Music Hall, 106–108 Cowley Rd,
Oxford OX4 1JE

First printing
1 3 5 7 9 10 8 6 4 2

A CIP catalogue record for this book
is available from the British Library

ISBN (pbk): 978-1-912408-44-3
ISBN (ebk): 978-1-912408-45-0

Designed by WatchWord Editorial Services, London
Typeset in Dante by www.twenty-sixletters.com

Printed and bound in Great Britain
by CPI Group (UK) Ltd, Croydon CR0 4YY

For Terry and Emile

2019

Ten. Nine. Eight. The old pier stands undressed, but
defiant still, and there's a boy in fingerless gloves who
does a cartwheel, and a girl with a face punctured by
piercings and a glittering in her eyes. The fireworks
squeal and light splendours on the water. Hey! Take
a photo, will ya? Seven. Six. Use the flash, the flash!
Five. And the dog wears one of those jackets that
I hope stops her being scared, and I have a whisky
tang on my tongue and a brine wash through my
hair, and the girl and boy kiss and the crowd goes
Ahhhhh cos a firework bursts wide open like a sun.
Four. Three. And the girl says, Who's your kiss for
tonight? and I say, James, he's with his wife, and she

laughs and says, It's like that, is it? Two. So the girl gives me her final tinny and she smiles at me and I can see what she would have looked like as a child, and then, Woah! Babe, cover your eyes! Cos a nude blur staggers across the pebbles and wades into the sea, and the sea pulls out its final breath of the year, a gutless wheeze, and slaps up against the naked old pier, which is only bones, and One, we are on the precipice of hope, again.

And a January where sleepers in seaside shelters kip on cardboard that held sun-swollen fruit. And then February, sodden with an empty promenade and a sky and sea melded the same, and our man plays clarinet against every morning's sleet. In like a lion, out like a lamb, March sloshes to April, upswelling open for the verdant plush of May and yoga on the Lawns, and barbecues that scorch pebbles and drift into the navy blue of the midnights. Blink, not so hard that you lose time, and it's June with flashing rain and marmalade skies. And then here it is, again.

Again, the longest day of the year. It's the day the sun stands still, a day for ancients and stones moved by miracles, and me.

Happy Birthday to me.

We get the face we deserve, that's what we're always told. To keep us good and honest and kind and small. I'm told I look younger than my age. People mean this as a compliment.

Really? Oh, thank you, I say, and I touch my cheek.

Peel back my skin though, and the truth idles everywhere: in glistening leg muscles and shoulder blades that could, if I say so myself, belong in an anatomy textbook. There's a truth in my never-inhabited uterus. In my fists. In a jagged crack that runs across my forearm, in a missing tooth lost at a disco, and a lost appendix, dug out from the abyss. Managed to keep both my kidneys, but I'd give one to the right person, and I've always kept my heart, cushioned close by offal, and persisting still. Tattery old heart holding all the years my face does not, and squeaking with so many truths it could be drawn on cave walls.

1972

I am born tiny and hairy. I am born silent and early. White coats and blue uniforms think I'm dead. So I'm smacked within an inch of my small croaking life, then placed on soft crocheted blankets in a glass box. They talk in percentages. The squeezed kind that don't yield profits or pass tests. Dad and Mum (because she is still around) bring in a man wearing a dog collar. He says prayers and he commits me to the underworld, and Boom! I turn from a puke yellow to pink and scream every profanity that I heard in the womb.

When Mum visits, she peers over me and she doesn't take off her coat. 'She's a ratty bugger. Don't think she wants to be here.'

'Bollocks!' Dad says, finding a chair.

But Mum is right: I pull out the tubes that support me and the blue uniforms sedate me. I scratch all I can reach, with fingernails the size of pinheads, until I bleed on the lambs' wool. Dad huffs on the glass and draws animals in his breath, while each miniature organ struggles. Dad says he can hear me screaming in the cafeteria three floors down, and when he finally brings me home, he doesn't sleep for a year.

Dad says I survived for an effing reason, believes I am destined for great things. Mum has moved on before I know what she thinks.

. . .

2019

The sun puddles on the bedroom floor at around 9am. Sometimes I am up at this time, usually I am not. I lie in bed waiting for something to change. I drink tea and eat toast until the dog threatens to wee.

This morning, talk radio says they're still coming over in their droves. Norman from Margate says enough is enough. He says the sooner we are out, the better.

The dog and I walk on the seafront, and every day the ocean is a different colour. Today it's a sage field, with a single drift of thin-thread turquoise that stretches from pier to pier.

And now, high on the promenade, is a large starfish that the dog is throwing at my feet.

'Leave it.'

She picks it up again, chucks it higher and it hits my shin before landing on the ground like an open hand. I nudge it with my foot and the dog, energised, flings it at me, relishing the game.

It belongs to the sea.

So I pick it up, and I hold the starfish between the tips of my forefinger and thumb, turning it back and forth. Up close it's possible to see its very fabric: an underside that's scaly and shark white, and a top half that's decorated in orange and pearls and prehistoric crust. Did you know a starfish can grow another body, create a whole different being, from a single, severed limb? Resurrection, it's quite the party trick.

I place it on the pebbles for the water to take, and my phone rings.

'Theatre. London,' my agent says, before I can say hello. 'You know that audition you went for. Few months back. Anyway, Elizabeth whatsherface had to pull out, broke her arm horse riding, bloody amazing.'

'Great.'

'And it's starring that Bright Young Thing—big buzz, wrapped a film with whatshisname. This is going to get a lot of attention, Cora. Do yourself a favour, bring your A game.'

1989

Old man pub. Sticky brown floor. A bloke is trying to chat me up. He asks me, almost hurt, as if he doesn't trust me, that isn't acting professionally lying? 'It's a sales job,' he says.

'Do I look like a shop girl?' and I spin around so he can see how wrong he's got it, because—doesn't he know—a few Snakey Bs down and squinting in the grubby light, I could be a chubby Anna Karina.

He leans back against the bar, eyes aglint, with a single dimple on his right cheek, which I notice pops when he's pleased.

'You're training to be a professional liar.' And the dimple digs in deeper, acts as an exclamation mark.

'No, I'm not,' I say, all earnest. 'It's the opposite, I'm trying to find truth.'

2019

It's just over an hour to get into London by train, cutting across the backs of people's gardens and patios, washing juddering on the lines.

Up early though, to run the dog dry on the seafront before I go, and talk radio has a heated debate this morning. Les from Aldershot says we need another vote, we didn't sign up for this, but Nina from West Wittering thinks that we are better off out, deal or no deal, that's the truth. That, let's face it, we are still being governed by foreigners, bullied by the mainland. The sea is glass-coloured, all refracted edges in the sun.

Out of the station, I wait ten minutes for a taxi. I don't mind. I never go on the Underground.

I worked in Soho once, when it was all neon and dark postcard naughtiness. Close your eyes and breathe deep, can you smell past skin? I can. Breathe deeper, through your mouth and nose, taste the faintness of Nescafé and boredom, feel the metal bed frame, the thin mattress.

Open your eyes.

Now, on the balcony opposite, there's a bloke having a fight with his boyfriend who's in the nip. In side streets, men stand with signs saying: *Gold for cash!* and *Increase your profits by 50%!* In the sunshine, tattoo parlours are opened by lilac and pink-haired girls with botanicals twining around thighs, and zoos of animals peeking out from denim shorts, climbing spines.

Down an alley, and Bright Young Thing is there, leaning against the wall near the stage door, vaping. She is tiny and scruffy, hair scraped back, with a face that's found with a Saturday job at a hairdressers or bakery. I saw her small part in a TV drama, and the trailer for the film though: out of the ordinariness unknowable lives are lived. In just ten minutes, she's cracked herself open to the broken parts we would all deny exist, and whole-hearted hardness and softness and sourness and sweetness is offered up.

'Hi, I'm Cora', I say.

And she says, 'Hey.'

She wipes her hand against her dungarees and I wish I had done the same because my hand is damp uncooked meat, which she notices when she reaches out and shakes it. I suspect she notices everything, she is built that way—notices, categorises, stores for later. What she doesn't know is that I am bricking it because, confession time, my CV is totally fudged. I haven't managed to get a theatre gig in years.

'Come on,' she says. 'I'll show you around.'

'How are you finding it all?'

'This is my dream, what I've always wanted.' And there is a loveliness to her naïveté. Her dreams will be outstripped by her reality, and if the critics are right, this will be only a footnote in her life.

She leads me down to the basement. And it's as if we're in the bow of a ship, because there are no windows, or natural light, or air, and the rest of the cast stand around, rinsed out. But when she enters, she switches from a young woman to The Actress and does what cannot be manufactured: she changes the quality of the room. Something happens, there's movement, people stand straighter, electrons become enthralled, practically visible.

'I see you've met.' Clive comes up and I wipe my hand down my trousers before shaking his. 'So delighted you could join at such short notice. I'm sure you are going to be fabulous, just fabulous.'

I don't say I have my doubts, because there's a prickle of something, maybe hope, growing inside me.

Clive claps his hands together. 'People,' he says, 'gather round. Form a circle. Start with me. La— La—Move your lips—La—La—La.' And we stand in this thin-skinned room, with tooth-coloured walls, making childlike sounds, and the strip lighting buzzes with homecoming.

1989

The Dimple is leaning against the bar. He takes a heavy pull on a cigarette and says, 'Truth?'

It is winter and glacial: icicles grow from drippy noses, eyebrows freeze. I'm seventeen and in my first year, living at the squat in the old children's hospital in Ealing. Drama school makes me ravenous, peeling back my bones to make me taste my marrow, and I have appetite for everything.

'It's like your own truth. What's inside you. If you dig deep enough.'

He is called Kit. He is seven years older than me and a cycle courier. 'So. What are you made of?' The dimple is as good as a smile.

'I don't know, yet.'

At the squat, Kit struts around my room. He knocks on walls and rubs plaster crumbs between his fingertips. He stands on his tiptoes and places his palm up against the damp ceiling. 'This place isn't good for you. I'm not being funny, it's not good for your health.'

'Aren't you cold?' I say.

He picks at a sodden exposed beam and shards of wood come off in his hand. 'See! Look at this.'

But I'm not interested in the building's structure. I'm in a sleeping bag under blankets and I'm watching him.

Naked, Kit doesn't have the leanness of a person who spends their days fast-pedalling around central London. He is squat and in profile looks like an S, all heavy stomach and fleshy bum, with a face that belongs on a country farm. His thighs are the only part of him that look like they belong on a bicycle— thick and double plaited with muscle, they are gifted from Atlas for the strongest of men.

'They condemned this place for a reason,' he says, and then to prove a point, the gods send gusts of wind that rattle the windows and snow finds its way through the roof to the holes in the ceiling and down to the floor.

'Use those saucepans, will you?'

Kit moves the pans and gets back into bed.

In the early morning, before there is any light and both of us lie apart and are strangers again, he says, 'I'm squatting at Cromer Street, near King's Cross. It's decent and dry, much nearer your school.' He stops, makes an empty cough. 'Join me if you want.'

'I'm happy here.'

Snow collects faster in the pots.

He shrugs. 'King's Cross, it's where it's all happening.'

Fancying someone feels like ulcers, or being trapped in a falling lift. It's an acceleration where nerves eat each other and hearts are held in teeth. Whatever this is, it's something else.

I place my finger in the dimple. 'It's so deep, it could eat my hand,' I say.

I visit Kit a few times in King's Cross and when the roof at the hospital is blown clean off and I wake to an unzipped night sky and a room lunar lit and unmoored, again he offers, more quietly than last time, and I move to Cromer Street.

Remember this: lives aren't shaped by ringed dates on the calendar. I know this now. Lives pivot on microseconds, on the tiniest wild seeds caught, discarded and forgotten, which grow at another time, in strange seasons, in years not yet imagined. For good or bad, lives can hinge entirely on distant genetics pulled through the ages, on upturned expressions of love, on a beautiful rare quirk found in another's face.

2019

'So, our play is a modern-day take on the Milgram Experiment of the 1960s, staged with an entirely female cast. What were everyone's initial takeaways from the text?' Clive makes eye contact with each one of us. 'Yes, Rachel?'

'It's about the power of authority, and our inbuilt resistance to defy it.'

Everyone nods.

'It's about questioning, and not questioning.'

'Yes.'

'Yes.'

Bright Young Thing opens her mouth to speak, and the room is wrung clean of any other sound, 'Within us all resides apathy to others.'

Clive nods obediently.

The air is thick with stillness and the smell of our bodies ripening and our breath souring, which should usher silence, but it doesn't. Instead, some old-forgotten muscle uncoils and shakes itself free.

I say, 'It's more than that, though. Isn't it agathokakological?' and the Bright Young Thing raises an eyebrow, and I am pleased. 'Are we not everything? We are good, and yet, there is a propensity for the darkest badness within us all.'

1989

June. A Tuesday, late evening. Kit and I lie on the sofa, sticky, limbs askew, all the windows open, and on the breeze King's Cross shows us its day of jollof rice and chicken, and coriander and rats, and wine and urine, and disinfectant and crushed almonds, and sex and skinned oranges.

Kit was right, but Kit's always right. King's Cross is where it's all happening. The world congregates here. Dealers and prostitutes with families, musicians, photographers, social workers and nurses. There's a rumour that at the same time every week a minister for something or other goes into one of the flats across the road, dressed as a copper.

There are noises in the night and cries that sometimes keep me awake. There are needles and blackened foil left in the walkways.

'Are you scared?' Kit asks. 'I would hate for you to be scared.'

And he asks because, despite bigging this place up, he often is. I catch him checking and double checking the locks on windows and doors and he sleeps with a screwdriver in our bed. He has even begun talking of moving, once I graduate, somewhere quiet with a village green.

'Are you sure you aren't scared?' he says again.

'I probably should be, shouldn't I? Sometimes, I definitely should be.'

But I'm not. I'm anything but. I am facing the sun and it is crystalline and blinding and all powerful.

At weekends, I join others and get into fisticuffs with the National Front on greasy pavements, and when Kit asks why, I tell him the truth: I say, 'Because it's important.' In the evenings, I work at the Pony Club, down one of the alleys off Brewer Street, and when I get in at 5am, after nine-hour shifts and walking home, passing the girls that are too young on Argyle Street, Kit is waiting up and fills saucepans with hot water and lemon peel and hand-picked lavender and sage, so I can soak my worn hands and feet.

2019

We are actioning. We are coming up with transitive verbs for how each of our characters hopes to influence others. My verbs so far:

Mock
Deride
Ensnare
Humour

Trouble
Defy

My character is called Iris and she is one of the helpers, encouraging the 'participants' to use the electric-shock buzzers. I am finding parts of Iris that used to belong in me.

Bright Young Thing loves experimenting with the verbs, rolling them around in her mouth, finding exactly the right ones:

Corroborate
Crucify
Outclass
Enmesh
Woo
Pledge
Antagonise

Clive pulls a face at antagonise. 'I'm not sure that's quite right. Does she antagonise? She's trying to push her agenda through.'

'But, Clive,' Bright Young Thing says, 'she understands antagonism is the only way to get heard.'

Maybe Bright Young Thing is beginning to understand how good she really is.

James is every shade of rich, but we always meet at a Travelodge out of town, in the afternoon, and every time we check in, it is the same young woman on reception. She speaks with an unidentifiable accent and she always wears a different name badge—last time she was Karolina, the time before, Zofia. This afternoon when we buzz, the door behind the reception opens and she stumbles out, sleep ruffled with claggy make-up and pillow lines on her face. Today, she is Sue.

James signs in. Mr and Mrs Portendorfer—a private joke—and he pays cash.

People feel shame for doing this. If I delve deep enough, I do too, but there are bigger things I feel shame for. So, I say, 'Hey. How you doing, today?'

James, who is already half-way down the corridor, turns.

Sue smiles and says, 'Well. I'm well, thank you.' She makes a point of glancing at our names in the register and then meeting my eye. 'Mrs Portendorfer, I do hope you enjoy your afternoon.'

The room is muted greys and maroons. The blinds hang heavy, blocking out the sunshine, and it's cool.

'Why are you always drawing attention to us?'

'I was just saying hello.'

We begin taking off our own clothes—we have never taken off each other's clothes. I'm haphazard, dress flung on the back of a chair, underwear still containing my shape on the floor, ready to be climbed back into. James folds everything, following the laundered creases, even on his socks, stacking them on the desk.

'Why though?' He takes off his watch and lines up his shoes so they are straight. Already, this is sex by numbers.

And then he gets into bed and flips me over, and as he winds his hand around my hair, he says, 'No matter how hard they try and clean these rooms, they're always dirty. Perhaps you can tell her that next time.'

Afterwards, I lie there and he falls asleep on me, and as I find the scar tissue on his body, the knots and ridges, he dreams, and I always think I know him better this way than in real life, because he dreams the way my dog does. He is always running, his body twitching against mine, as he makes tiny animal sounds. Sometimes, he cries and his DNA streaks across my skin. When he wakes, I want to ask him about who he sees, but he looks to the wall, to the bathroom, to the door, he talks about irritating clients, our steadfast government. The first time it happened, I said, 'Bad dream?' and he said, 'Cora, Cora, Cora, don't you know, dreams are the very last vestige of privacy.'

2018

Outside, the night is wholly black. Last train home and inside the carriage is bleached yellow by lights made for hospitals or police stations. There are two of us here. Me and the man opposite, the one with public-school-boy hair even though he looks a bit older than me. I'm on my way back from visiting Kit and his wife, Lark. We see each other a few times a year now and they have recently moved out of their big Northern city apartment to a stone wall cottage, in a silent hamlet. During the day, we hiked parts of the Pennine Way, and in the evening, Lark made an intricate meal from scratch. Kit assisted: he chopped and grated and stirred, and at every opportunity he would kiss her shoulder or circle her waist, and it was clear our shared history, which I held so close, and which he too had held for a while, has evaporated for him.

The man on the train notices the dog before me, and she goes to him the way she goes to everyone. He pats her and when she lies on her back, he stoops down and tickles her.

'Name?' he says.

'Her name is Nugget.'

'And what's your name?'

And when I tell him, he says, 'Cora, Cora, Cora. It's a call from deep within, isn't it? Rather than a name.'

And I think, yeah it is, and no one has ever noticed that before.

James owns some security firm, he's ex-army, he tells me over dinner a couple of nights later. He served in places that dominated the news in the nineties, when genocide became a live event again. I want to ask what that was like.

But instead, it takes three dates and texts answered at strange times for me to ask if he is married. He tells me he has no intention of leaving his wife, not while his kids are so young, but he wants a connection, he wants some fun. I need some fun. God, I need some fun.

1989

Early September, skin is sun-full, heat still soars and blisters. Our Eritrean neighbour from the squat next door, resplendent in white and gold and henna, got married this afternoon.

We wheel a sound system out into the courtyard, and burly boys stand by to make sure it isn't nicked. The whole block is out. There are trestle tables covered with cloth, the colours of emerald and sapphire, and laden with dozens of plates and bowls of injera and doro wat, and jam jars filled with tea lights.

We eat until our stomachs are stretched tight and then the music starts. Drums herald beginnings, a kraar cascades lifting and spinning notes. We sway, raise our arms, and our hands chase the music in the air. Someone has a video camera, hoisted high on to their shoulder to capture the entire occasion. He makes sure he films every single person, and we all jostle into frame. He hopes one day to return and show it to the folks back home.

That night, we fall into bed. Kit, baked and full and pickled, says, 'You ever thought this could be us? We could get somewhere with more space, a garden, a house with more than four walls.'

I pretend to be asleep and when Kit passes out, I lie in the darkness and say, 'Kitty Kat, you should know me by now, I need a home with no walls.'

2019

We are on our feet and blocking. We move around the room with our scripts and pencils in hand, finding the right positions to express the undercurrents. Bright Young Thing moves slower than the rest of us, finding the exact space to fill, even the way her feet turn in is precise. I imagine her toes, wiggling in her scruffy trainers, are finding their home in each scene. Her ears, her elbows, everything becomes transformation.

'She's gifted,' Clive whispers. 'I mean, astonishingly gifted.'

In a different time, a lifetime ago, people used to think that about me.

. . .

2002

My agent says we should scrap my IMDb profile. 'Come on,' she says. 'You're better than this. I mean, didn't you win that prize in your first year?'

Later, Kit looks it up. IMDb's third entry for me: *Lady eating doughnuts*.

2019

We're back at the Travelodge. James seems to have more time on his hands, and there's an old white man in reception. Karolina/Zofia/Sue has disappeared. The old man looks us up and down and practically throws the key card.

'Thank God,' James says, when we get into the room, folding his trousers. 'No more aimless conversations.'

'Okay then,' I say. 'Tell me about Bosnia.'

'Take off your clothes.'

'I want to know.' I sit on the edge of the bed. 'What was it like?'

'Cora. Come on. Get in.' He reaches for me.

I look at him and it's odd magic: I can see him properly for the first time. 'Did you kill anyone?'

'Why do people always want to know that? It's war. Come on—I like it when you're angry. You like it too.' He tries pulling off my shirt.

'I want to know.'

He stops, maybe seeing me for the first time. 'Are we going to fuck?' he says.

'No.'

He sighs, as if I have broken a spell, and as he rolls over and reaches for the remote control, he says, 'Fuck off, then.'

I lie in my own bed and outside is the spill of life: lights of take-away delivery drivers and taxis. The clack of heels, the chatter of girls, the thump and roar of the band at the bar around the corner. I get up, put clothes over pyjamas, a lead on the dog, and begin walking. James texts and says he is sorry. His wife and kids are away and would I like to come and stay the night? He'll make it up to me.

I keep walking. Past the pier and clubs emptying of teenagers with gleaming faces, past the old Victorian lift, the tea rooms, towards the chalky white cliffs. I walk until the light begins—the sea is so far out this morning, it's undressed the shore. It's taken the pebbles and rocks and left the soft, sandy underbelly.

. . .

It's my turn to host them both, but Kit rings me the day before they are due to arrive and says Lark can't make it. 'Aw, really? What a shame.' And I shove the rosé shit to the back of the cupboard.

I hope, without his wife there, we can make a play for friendship, expose the bricks of secret space and language that belonged just to us, but when he arrives late, he concentrates on the dog, playing with her and fussing her so she lies on her back, and sticks her legs in the air.

'Let's get out of here,' he says.

We go to the egg-blue tearoom with mismatched cups and saucers and our favourite scones, ones with raisins for me, no raisins for Kit, and the only jam Kit likes: apricot. I order so that he sees that I remember. We walk along the seafront and back to the flat. After we moved from the squat, this was our flat, used to be our flat.

'Can you believe I'm still here?'

But Kit flicks through his old albums. 'Mind if I take these?'

In the evening, I find flour and make a well, the egg viscous in my hands. He helps, holding the dough, as I roll it through the pasta maker, squashing it thinner and thinner, until it's an almost-translucent sheet. Normally, I don't cook. I eat cereal most evenings, but it's a peculiar quirk—I'm pretty good at pasta.

We let the pasta dry a little and drink wine. I sit on my galley kitchen sideboard, while he perches on the stool.

'Hey,' I say, 'remember that time, you came back with that bloke to Cromer Street, and he'd taken something or other, and you ended up resuscitating him in the middle of the courtyard?'

'Yeah, I remember.'

'And a whole bunch of people came out and gave you a round of applause.'

'I said, I remember.'

We sit down to eat and I light a few candles, but he blows them out, turns the light back on. 'I want to see what I'm eating.'

But he doesn't eat. Not really.

We're halfway through, in silence, nothing I say sticks.

Kit turns the pasta over and cuts it into pieces that cannot be twirled around a fork. He builds it into a mound and pushes his knife through it again.

'What's going on?'

He puts his cutlery down. 'I need to stop the money. Not straight away, but in the next few months. Lark and I…we're pregnant.'

I actually laugh. 'You're too old.'

He watches me, waiting.

Then, when I realise he's serious, I say, 'You said you didn't want kids.'

'No, you said you didn't want kids. Congratulations might be nice.'

'I'll crack open the champagne.'

'We'll just wind it down slowly. I don't want to leave you short,' he says.

'I depend on that money.'

'Well, maybe it's time to find a proper job. Something that pays.'

I look at the damp patch of mould near his head.

'I can't afford it. We can't afford it,' he says more gently. 'It will be okay. This is what you need. This'll get your life back on track.'

I imagine them lying in bed discussing the best way to tell me. Him not wanting to hurt me, her saying he owes me nothing.

'Don't tell me what I need.'

He stops for a second. 'Corrie. You always want the truth. It's been years—'

'Stop. Can we stop this conversation?'

'I did my best—'

The bricks I wanted to see are now exposed, and whatever we once had has crumbled. New walls and roads and cities and stories have been built between us. And he has cut up the meal I made for him into mouthfuls for a child.

2004

Fig trees and lemon groves, a white cottage with blue steps, cool tiles under foot. Our own private swimming pool, the size of a large bath.

On star-sprinkled nights, we walk down the hill to the taverna, we eat charcoaled tuna steaks and salads and wander back up the hill, and I insist we make love every night, and I think maybe, finally, I can be happy. Kit believes we are finally happy.

But during the day when he hikes or reads, I spend my time in the eye of the fierce Greek sun until I hurt, and then I sit cross-legged at the bottom of the giant bath, and I do my crying underwater.

. . .

2009

Kit hurriedly pulls off his jumper, his shirt, his thermals, and then throws on similar, but fresh clothes. His breath plumes in chalky grey dust, before it evaporates. I'm doing the same. The boiler has been broken since last summer. By morning, there will be ice swilling around the bottom half of the window.

'How's work?'

'Fine.' He pulls on the second jumper.

'I've got an audition for *Midsomer Murders*.'

'Don't tell me, another big break, right?'

We get into bed, which is a small double, but there is still acres of room between us.

And now, under the duvet with socks and a woolly hat on, all curled up and foetal-shaped, I am in the hinterlands of sleep. Deliciously close.

It's a featured part, I think. I'll buy a steak dinner if I get it, that'll teach him, he'll literally eat my words.

He coughs an empty cough, and it pulls me back from sleep, and I am about to say something when he says, 'What are we doing?' And his voice sounds like it belongs to someone else.

'What do you mean?' But I know exactly what he means.

'Do you love me?' he says.

'Why are we together?' he says.

'What do you mean?' I say again. My feet and legs are numb, they are dissolving into the bed. I think my body is disappearing too.

Kit has his back to me. Wearing the jumper I gave him for Christmas a few years ago.

'Look at me. Please.'

I hear him breathe. 'I can't.'

'Please.'

And he turns.

'Are you leaving me?' The street lamp outside shines light in the room, but if I held up my hand I wonder if I could see it or whether it too has vanished. I take it out from under the covers, I touch his face.

'Is that what you want?' he says.

'No.' And then, 'I don't know.' Because hasn't this gone on long enough? I put my hand away, but he reaches under the duvet, picks it up and places it back on his face.

We stagger on for another month, and every hour we have, we are honest and furious and tender with each other. We are tethered to each other by weighted strings that are snipped and hastily re-tied back together and snipped again, by one or both of us. We are close again, so close that nightly I sob and he just doesn't sleep. A month like this. Then he moves in with Lark. Fifteen years younger than him, with two degrees in business and accounting, and a face unwanting for anything in life.

2019

9am. The puddle of sunshine grows on the carpet, bleaching it to bone. Kit brings me a cup of tea before he leaves.

'You'll still come and stay, won't you? Lark would love to see you. You can meet the baby.'

'Of course,' I say.

After I hear the click of the front door, I get up and go into the living room. He's neatly folded the bedding, the pillowcase with a single hair caught in its fabric. I remake his bed and get in. I lie in it a while, his smell of barbershop shaving cream and ash, and then I ring James and say, 'Are you still up for a visitor?'

1990

On Thursday and Saturday nights I work at the Pony Club—a place of feathers and the darkest velvet. I'm a hostess—I show customers to their booths, up-lit with soft lighting, or to forbidden rooms behind heavy brocade curtains.

Early February and a producer from America walks over. 'You. You act? They said you act.'

'I'm training. I'm on scholarship.'

'Your Mrs Thatcher says there are too many actors.'

'I heard that she doesn't think much of producers either.'

'Feisty, eh? Come sit with us, because this is how films get made, Feisty. In glorified strip clubs. Trying to convince the money men.'

I sit with him and his three friends in a booth the colour of forests, as they argue about financing and shooting films seventies style.

'No more guns and tits. Who wants guns and tits? Yeah, Max, I know you do. Undercurrent, I want undercurrent.'

He turns to me. 'I'm from Wyoming. It's all undercurrent there.'

'I live in King's Cross. It's all overspill.'

And he looks at me closer and turns to Max. 'What do you think? Cora as Imelda.'

The other man stares at me. 'Her nose,' he says. 'I don't know…'

The Producer places his index finger under my chin and turns my face to the side. And then says, 'Imelda doesn't have to be beautiful. How did those LA castings go? Trust me on this one. You about this week, Cora?'

2019

The taxi crawls along the road, the driver and I both looking for James's house because James lives in a world with high fences and no numbers, only names.

And then, here it is, and James lives in a house that from the outside looks like one of those residences they hire for an Agatha Christie film: a 1920s art deco mansion, white with pillars and palm trees and a balcony on the first floor overlooking the drive.

James takes an age to open the door, and when he does, it's clear he's started early. Sickly sweet ferment rises off him; it's in my nose, I can taste it on my tongue.

'Welcome to the soon-to-be-famous actress.'

'Hardly.'

He makes a grandiose sweep with his hands to the insides of the house. Despite the brightness outside, it's dark, and what little light there is shows there is nothing. It takes a few seconds to realise, but this is a house stripped—no photos on the walls, only picture hooks. It doesn't seem like a home; it's just a grander Travelodge.

'Shall we go to the park?' I say.

'No, no, you're here now. Might as well make the most of the facilities.' As if it's a spa. And his voice is trapped in the hall, bouncing hard between the ceiling and floor.

He takes the wine and strawberries I've brought, and places them on a side table, then entwines his fingers through mine and leads me up the sweep of the winding stairs to the landing.

'I didn't think you'd come,' he says. And he kisses my neck, his tongue traces my lips. 'Cora, Cora, Cora.'

'Do I get a tour? Why don't you give me the tour?' My voice is quiet.

He continues kissing my eyelids, across my forehead, down my cheekbones, and again to my lips, gently biting my lower lip. I don't like the tender James. I like it less when he takes off each item of my clothing slowly, placing them one at a time on the balustrade, until I am naked. He lies me down on the carpet before taking off his clothes. He looks me in the eye and says we are making love. I know where I am with angry James—I like his anger. This James is playing out a fantasy of which I am no part.

I want him to sleep and become the feral animal that scratches and quivers, but when it's finished, he puts on his boxers immediately, and says, 'How about a drink then?' and goes downstairs.

By the time I arrive in the kitchen—huge, white, marbled, emptied—I wonder if he's squatting, whether it's a façade.

'So, little Cora. What do you make of my palace?'

'Where is everything?'

'You know. Gone.'

The bottle of wine I brought is on the side. He opens it and tops up his glass.

'Steady, James.'

He wiggles the bottle at me.

'No thanks.'

'How's that play going?'

'Good. Previews next week.'

'Any freebie tickets?'

And when I don't answer, he says, 'You've probably guessed, the wife has gone. Left me for her PT, didn't she?'

Good for her, I think.

'She's taken the kids. My kids.'

'I should go.'

He burps and bangs his chest with a fist. 'No, no. You've just got here, Cora…'

'No, I'll go.'

'Cora. Cora. I feel fucking dreadful. Help me to bed.'

He slings his arm over my shoulder and we stagger down the hall, my sandals clopping on the horrible tiles. Up the stairs, and I find what must have been his and his wife's bedroom, bare and all white.

'Come on.' I gently push him through the room and he stumbles onto the bed.

When Kit and I were first looking for flats, the estate agent took us to a different part of town. A place where we could afford a whole house. 'It's been repossessed, but don't let that put you off! Three bedrooms and a thirty-foot garden.' But it was bleaker than a temporary squat—Christmas decorations boxed and left in the middle of the living room, a child's tiny action figure lying on its side on the stairs.

But James's wife managed to take everything, lamps gone from the bedside tables, the bathroom cabinet swept clean. Across the hall, there's a small bedroom in light blue—a train border chugging around the walls—the only sign that a child was ever here.

Another bedroom, an older kid, maybe. A book-case emptied, the wardrobe doors open, grains of dirt where shoes once were.

Next door is a study. The only part of the house that looks lived in—papers stacked up, a computer. To the back is a slim black cabinet. I pause, a ticking in my head. I go over and open it.

And there at the bottom of the cabinet is a hunting rifle.

'I miss it.'

James is behind me. His arms circle around my waist. Still drunk but strong.

'I miss being a soldier.'

'You should keep it locked up,' I say. And I untangle myself from him and move to leave the room.

'You want to know what it's like, war. To kill someone. Isn't that your question?'

I'm at the door. 'No, I want to know how you survived killing people.'

And he picks up the rifle. Tosses it from one hand to the other. 'Why?'

'Because I do.'

'There's a better reason than that. Tell me.'

He smiles and licks his lips, and the air changes. 'Come on, Cora. Is this for a role?' And then he holds the gun up and takes aim, pointing it straight at me.

Everything has slowed.

He cocks it.

'Tell me, Cora.'

I say, 'Because I've done bad things too.'

'Go on,' he says.

But I say nothing.

So, he pulls the trigger.

Click.

Nothing.

And I wait for a second. A whole fucking second. And then I run. And run. And run.

Into a Saturday afternoon. One of those gloriously late Indian summer days, dipped in gold, that belong to barelegged teenagers and getting gentle sunstroke in the garden.

. . .

1980

Hands mittened in the prefab. I was allowed to look after the rabbits over the October half-term, and now I want to play Mary, but I bet Linda-Claire will get the part because she is pretty and has both parents. But she has bright blonde hair and everyone knows Mary was dark haired. And also, I always put up my hand in class.

Mrs Kenny says I'm poxy Shepherd Number Two, and I say I don't want to be Shepherd Number Two, I want to be Mary, and Mrs Kenny tries to ignore me, but I say I would make a great Mary, that my father thinks I'm destined for great things.

And Mrs Kenny says, 'Cora Vincent, I don't know what rubbish your tinker father's been filling your head with, but I think what happened to those poor rabbits shows us you would make a most unfit Mary.' She shakes her head. 'Wicked girl.'

I don't tell her we were hungry. Instead, I say, 'My father's no tinker, he's a horse dealer.' Then I look at my desk and I say, quietly, though I make sure it's loud enough for her to hear, 'And he says you're an eejit.'

I look up. Mrs Kenny is bright red. She calls me up to the front of the room, gets the cane out, and says, 'You're going to the headmaster's after this for more of the same.' She says 'wicked' twelve more times, and each time she strikes me with the cane harder than the last.

2019

The ocean is slate today, with lacey frills. They came down on the train over the weekend with piping and pieces of wood. The litter pickers are still out clearing the rubbish. There's ripped cardboard signs, tinnies, further along the promenade, a lone police helmet and piles of horse shit, and then further still, near where the dog and I turn to wander home, a long slick of aging blood, dried and dark brown. Worse than last time.

The sea won't come up this far, the rain will have to clear it, whenever that will be, and by then they will have come down again for another rumble.

I step around the blood, but the dog is straining to get a sniff. Brian from Edgeware is on the radio. He says the people have spoken. He says no deal. And yes, yes, he voted for UKIP, and yes, he'd do it again, and no, he's not racist, and then he says something I haven't heard in a while—not since the days the National Front were knocking about King's Cross.

He says England is for the English.

1996

I'm at Pinewood for four days. Fantasy sci-fi. I'm a troll. The lead actor is so high he throws sandwiches at me, thinking I'm a hallucination. I stay at a B'n'B that's beige and flocked and run by a woman called Lilith. Every evening, on my return to chilly sheets, the sky washed in pink and pearl, I slow a little as I pass under the viaduct to read it, to absorb the hope: *Give peas a chance.*

2019

We have a final rehearsal today and then a preview. Bright Young Thing is plastered on the side of buses and on breakfast telly. Tickets for tonight have all sold out. She's only contracted for the first run, but bigger theatres are sniffing round with longer contracts for the rest of us.

When I arrive in London, there are no taxis. A mainline water pipe has burst and whole areas outside the station are closed off.

'Your best bet is the Underground, love,' the station attendant tells me. 'Honestly, they're going to be jammed up for hours.'

I step on to the descending escalator, each chamber of my heart working harder, pump, pump, pump, until I thrum. There are so many people; there were always too many people. In front are women in suits, and workmen in dark blue aertex shirts and shorts. There are young people with headphones clamped over their ears. No ceiling above, and wires hang down, and on the wall is a row of descending television screens, each showing the same picture for five seconds, before the next, on a loop.

I step off the escalator and move towards the platform.

1990

Saturday. I'm meeting the Producer tonight, but still for the craic I go to a corner of London where we've heard they're gathering—with their flags and fourteen-hole DMs. We outnumber them, just, but we know they'll have metal and wood. So we stop at the breakers yard and pick up some piping. I get one with a bit of weight.

They stand in front of us, all skinned and raging at us. And we stand and shout back. A few police hang around. We move at the same time and the coppers just move out of the way.

There is a power in righteousness, a pureness that needs to be guarded, because otherwise it becomes something else. I hit him hard with the piping—he is younger than me, he looks frightened: we were all children once—his eyes widen, seem to change from blue to brown, blood collects around his ear. Then I hit his mate, more seasoned, who hits me back. So, I hit the older man harder still, something animal grows inside me, something that needs quelling, one more hit, and one more still, and he crumples. He raises his arm to protect himself, palms up. Small hands, I remember the crack of the piping on his girlish hands. One more. One more still. And then we can hear the sirens and it's over and we all run.

And later I'm standing on the platform, all cleaned up and ready for the Pony Club and the Producer, and

I can feel all my edges now and it's mental here cos it's Saturday night and everyone's done up in heels and suits and still some shoppers with their bags are out and others are going home from work. So I don't see them. The pair from before. But they see me. They wait until the tube carriage is rolling in. They wait until it's just a few feet away from me. They come at me from both sides, bystanders later tell the police. And in that moment, that microsecond, a woman, jostled by the crowds, steps out in front of me, toes over the yellow line. She is in red, I remember the bold red of her coat. And when I am driven into her, when they drive me into her, and before she falls and her life just vanishes forever, my cheek brushes up against her coat which is wool and I remember the surprise because the wool is so rough on my skin and I didn't know wool could be rough like that.

The church is rammed. I turn up and stand at the back. From the papers, I find out her name was Anna. She was a mother. She was married to Greg. He's a plumber.

On her coffin is a photo, different from the one run in the press—it's a photo of her with her two kids, from a summer gone. The three of them in a paddling pool in the garden, her dark, curly hair laid flat by the water.

Kit told me not to come, said it wouldn't help anyone, but I want to hear who she really is. Sometimes I can't hear for the crying, and even though nothing bad is said at funerals, she was all good and kind and honest, the best of ordinary.

No one blames me, except maybe her mother. Her mother would push me on the line herself, if it would bring her daughter back. I don't blame her; I've thought about it a few times, and all.

2019

We have a few hours between final rehearsal and the first preview.

Final rehearsal went well. Bright Young Thing is hypnotising, but Clive comes up to me afterwards and says I hold my own. 'You've surprised me,' he says.

And now I can't sit still in the dressing room.

So I walk around Soho, and end up stumbling on a street I've avoided. Another street I worked on, after I got fired from the Pony Club, and after I dropped out of drama school. I worked at the top of a very narrow staircase. I was there a month before Kit found me. He punched the man to get me out and the man's nose doubled in size and was a bloody mess. Kit put his coat on me and buttoned it up. He put his arm around me and took me down the stairs and brought me barefooted back to the squat. It was the fifth time he'd had to come find me. We moved to Brighton shortly after that.

1989

Old man pub. Sticky brown floor. The bartender has called time already and is collecting glasses. My friends have gone—we have classes early in the morning. The Dimple stands and brushes ash off his jeans.

'Walk you, Cora?'

'Sure.'

'So, where do you live?'

'The old children's hospital.'

He raises an eyebrow.

'What?' I laugh.

'It's falling apart.'

We walk out into frozen sleet and London streets painted in ice, with a wind that rolls bins down the road. We walk into a cold that wants to eat our faces, and snow that blows through our bodies. From up his sleeve, a tinny that he has filched from the pub. He taps the top.

'Share it?' he says, and he peels back the ring pull and gives me first swig. 'Do you want to be famous?'

'Ha! Nah, I just want to know stuff.'

'Truth?'

'Yeah.'

'About what?'

I stop in yellow-lighted darkness, and he can't see how bright my eyes are, but they must be bright because I feel so alive. At this moment, I feel electrified by all of life, and I say, 'Everything. I just want to know the truth about everything.'

Acknowledgements

Thank you to Creative Future, Myriad Editions and New Writing South, and specifically Matt Freidson, Candida Lacey and Lesley Wood for this fantastic opportunity. Still pinching myself! Many thanks also to Laura Wilkinson for her wonderful mentoring, and Vicki Heath Silk for her thoughtful and patient editing.

Thank you to my gang Emski, Mags, Momo, Kiki, Lou, Steve S, Ginie, Pies, Ames, Hen and Gini for keeping me afloat and being ace. To the Two Toms (L and V) for encouragement, and Julie and Neil for keeping me writing. To Oonagh for support. To Helen S for unrivalled kindness. Thank you to Emile, Willie and Nat for being unbreakable, and to Terry for always believing in me, even and especially when I never believed in myself.

About the author

Georgina Aboud is an award-winning short story writer. Her previous work on international development issues, where she specialised in gender, climate change and food security, has taken her around the world. She has observed elections in Kosovo, Macedonia and Ukraine, collaborated with forest and mountain communities in India and Colombia, worked on briefing papers in Bangladesh, and pulled pints in Peru. She lives in Hove, East Sussex.

About Spotlight

Spotlight Books is a collaboration between Myriad Editions, Creative Future and New Writing South to discover, guide and support writers whose voices are under-represented.

Our aim is to spotlight new talent that otherwise would not be recognised, and to help writers who face barriers, or lack opportunities, to develop their creative and professional skills in order to create a lasting legacy of work.

Each of our three organisations is dedicated to specific aspects of writer development. Together we are able to offer a clear ladder of support, from mentorship through to development editing and promotional opportunities.

Spotlight books are not only treasures in themselves but also beacons to other under-represented writers. For further information, please visit: www.creativefuture.org.uk

Spotlight is supported by Arts Council England.

'These works are both nourishing and inspiring, and a gift to any reader.'—Kerry Hudson

Spotlight stories

Georgina Aboud
Cora Vincent

Tara Gould
The Haunting of Strawberry Water

Ana Tewson-Božić
Crumbs

Spotlight poetry

Jacqueline Haskell
Stroking Cerberus: Poems from the Afterlife

Elizabeth Ridout
Summon

Sarah Windebank
Memories of a Swedish Grandmother